The Night Iceberg

Helen Stephens

ALISON
GREEN
BOOKS

Tofta was cross.

That was **her** Jack Rabbit that the baby was chewing.

And that was **her** favourite storybook that the baby was scrunching.

Her mummy said she had to learn to share.

But this was **her** very own bedroom that the baby was going to be sleeping in now.

"I don't **want** to share!" said Tofta. But she had to.

That night, an iceberg floated past Tofta's bedroom window and stopped. It looked peaceful and beautiful. It looked as if it didn't belong to anyone.

"That's going to be my iceberg," Tofta thought. "And I'm not going to share it with anyone."

She thought about what she'd need on the iceberg:
her favourite jumper (which was really her dad's),
her Jack Rabbit, her best fishing net – and a tin of
sardines, in case she wasn't very good at fishing.

Then she tip-toed down the path
and jumped onto her iceberg.

The iceberg drifted out to sea.

Tofta danced around happily.
At last she had something
that was just for her.

But then . . .

Pit-pat,

pit-pat,

pit-pat,

pit-pat,

pit-pat!

"Go away!" said Tofta.
"This is **my** iceberg."

The penguin looked
as if he thought it
was **his** iceberg.

They both sulked for a bit.

Tofta started to feel hungry.
She tried to catch some fish,
but they were too slippy,
so she opened her tin of sardines.

Pit-pat, pit-pat, pit-pat.

"Go away!" said Tofta.
"These are my sardines.

"Oh, all right. Just one, then."
They had one sardine each.

The penguin nuzzled Tofta's arm.
That felt nice.

"You can be my friend," said Tofta,
"but you can't have my last sardine.
I'm saving that."

All of a sudden, the penguin dived into the sea.

"Where are you going?"
cried Tofta.

Then she heard:

pit-pat,

pit-pat,

pit-pat,

pit-pat,

pit-pat,

pit-pat,

pit-pat,

pit-pat,

pit-pat,

pit-pat!

It was five hundred penguins!

And they all wanted Tofta's sardines!

"But I've only got one left!" cried Tofta. Reluctantly, she gave it to the littlest penguin.

The littlest penguin snuggled up to her to say thank you.
He felt very soft and fluffy. Tofta gave him a cuddle.

That felt so nice, that Tofta made a big decision.
She said to all the penguins: "Would you like to share my iceberg?
I can show you my sliding game."

The penguins were very good
at Tofta's sliding game.
They played for hours.

At last everyone was tired, so they all gathered round and Tofta told them a story. It was about a little girl who had a mum, and a dad, and a baby brother . . .

and how she sailed away one night on her very own iceberg which she shared with lots of penguins. They played together until the little girl was tired. And she said:

"I want to go home now!"

But it was dark and cold and she didn't know the way.

So the penguins tucked her up in her great big jumper, and Jack Rabbit and the littlest penguin snuggled up to keep her warm.

Then all the penguins dived into the sea, and guided the iceberg back through the night . . .

... and right through till dawn,

all the way home ...

. . . to where her very own baby brother was asleep in
their room. Tofta tiptoed over to her brother's cot,
and put Jack Rabbit in beside him.

"Wake up!" she whispered.
"I have to tell you all about my iceberg!"

This book was inspired by a trip to London Zoo where I drew the penguins. I liked their solemn expressions, and the way they silently followed each other round the edge of the pool. At feeding time they would get very excited, but in the very quiet way that only penguins can do. I thought they would make great characters in a book.

Not long after, I read a story by Tove Jansson who wrote the *Moomin* books. The story was about a little girl who sees an iceberg drift up to her island. She runs down to meet it and thinks about jumping on, but the moment passes. I wondered what would happen if the girl did jump on. The two ideas came together and — hey presto! *The Night Iceberg* was born!

Helen Stephens

To Holly, Poppy and Frieda

First published in 2010 by
Alison Green Books
An imprint of Scholastic Children's Books
Euston House, 24 Eversholt Street
London NW1 1DB
A division of Scholastic Ltd
www.scholastic.co.uk
London – New York – Toronto – Sydney – Auckland
Mexico City – New Delhi – Hong Kong

HB ISBN: 978-1-407107-90-5
PB ISBN: 978-1-407107-91-2

Rockhopper penguin London Zoo